SAM SILVER: UNDERCOVER PIRATE

THE GHOST SHIP

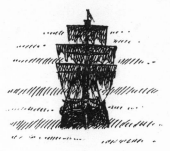

THE GHOST SHIP

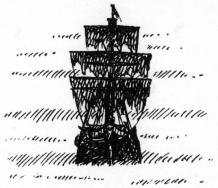

Jan Burchett and Sara Vogler

Illustrated by Leo Hartas

Orion
Children's Books

First published in Great Britain in 2012
by Orion Children's Books
a division of the Orion Publishing Group Ltd
Orion House
5 Upper St Martin's Lane
London WC2H 9EA
An Hachette UK company

1 3 5 7 9 10 8 6 4 2

Text copyright © Jan Burchett and Sara Vogler 2012
Map and interior illustrations copyright © Leo Hartas 2012

A catalogue record for this book is
available from the British Library.

ISBN 978 1 4440 0585 1

Printed in Great Britain by Clays Ltd, St Ives plc

For 'Webman',
our website superhero – aka Alan Tindley.

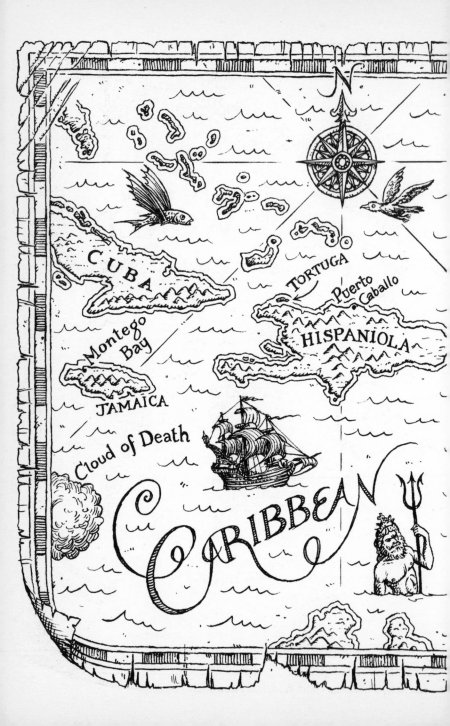

N

CUBA

Montego
Bay

JAMAICA

Cloud of Death

TORTUGA
Puerto
Caballo

HISPANIOLA

CARIBBEAN

The
SEA
WOLF

Captain's
Cabin

Hammocks

Gun Deck

Galley

Ship's Stores

CHAPTER ONE

It was a rainy Monday morning and Sam Silver was getting ready for school. But he wasn't happy about it.

"I can't believe Mr Nodsworthy has banned football for a whole week," he grumbled to himself. "Just because someone booted the ball and flattened Class Four's tomatoes."

Then an idea shot into his head like

a cannonball. He knew how to cheer himself up. He snatched an old bottle from his shelf and shook out an ancient gold doubloon.

Sam was always finding interesting objects on the beach at his home in Backwater Bay but this sand-pitted bottle was extra special. Not only had he found a gold coin inside but he'd also discovered a letter from an ancestor of his, a fierce pirate called Joseph Silver. The letter had told him where a great hoard of treasure lay and when he'd rubbed the coin an amazing thing had happened. He'd been whisked back more than three hundred years to 1706 and joined the crew of a really cool pirate ship, the *Sea Wolf!* Captain Blade and his brave men liked nothing better than sailing the Caribbean to find treasure, so they'd all set off straight away.

Sam decided to see what the pirates were up to right now. And he didn't have to

worry that his mum and dad would miss
him and start sending out search parties –
not one second passed in the present while
he was being a buccaneer.

Sam quickly changed out of his school
uniform into the tatty jeans and T-shirt
he'd worn on the *Sea Wolf*. He didn't dare
risk getting his uniform all ripped and
torn! His mum would go mad.

He rubbed the coin on his sleeve and
waited for the dizzy feeling he'd felt last
time he'd been whisked away into the past.
Nothing happened. He rubbed it harder
but still found himself sitting on his bed.
Sam stared miserably at the doubloon.
Perhaps it only worked once and he'd
never find himself on board
the *Sea Wolf* ever again. His
heart sank to his trainers.

Then he remembered
– last time he'd spat
on the coin before he

rubbed it. Perhaps he needed Silver spit to make it work. He decided to give it a try . . .

All around him Sam's bedroom walls set off in a fast spin. There was a deafening rush of air and he had the feeling he was being sucked into a giant vacuum cleaner. He closed his eyes in delight.

"*Sea Wolf*, here I come!" he shouted.

Sam landed with a thud on a hard wooden floor and opened his eyes.

Awesome! He was in the storeroom on board the pirate ship just like last time.

But before he could move, his ears were split by the loudest scream he'd ever heard.

A girl with roughly chopped hair and pirate breeches was standing over him, shrieking at the top of her voice.

It was his friend Charlie. Sam staggered to his feet. She must have seen him pop up out of nowhere. How was he going to explain that?

Charlie grabbed a mop. "The ghost of

Sam Silver!" she yelled, trying to whack
him over the head with it. "Come back to
haunt us! Get away from me, you horrible
spook!"

"I'm not a ghost," said Sam, dodging
the wet mop head.

"Oh, yes you are," said Charlie, waving
it in his face. "When you disappeared in
the middle of the ocean the crew said you
must have drowned. And now a week later
you appear out of thin air! No mortal

being can do that. Be gone, you fiend from hell!"

"You've got it wrong—" Sam began.

"I thought you were my friend," Charlie went on crossly, chasing him round the storeroom. "Friends don't come back and scare each other when they're dead."

The wet mop slapped down on his head.

"Yuck!" cried Sam, wiping his eyes. "Look, if I was a ghost that would have gone straight through me, wouldn't it?"

Charlie looked at the water dripping off Sam's nose. "I suppose so," she said doubtfully.

"I really am alive," insisted Sam.

"Ahoy there, Charlie," came a shout from the deck above, "are you all right?"

For a moment it looked as if Charlie was going to call for help.

"You must believe me," Sam pleaded.

"Charlie!" came the shout again. "What be the matter?"

· 14 ·

"All's well," Charlie called back. "I'll be up soon." She put down the mop. "You've got some explaining to do, Sam Silver," she said. "One minute I'm in here looking for sail thread and the next minute you appear at my feet with a stupid grin on your face."

Sam took a deep breath. There was only one thing for it. He had to tell her the truth.

He peered out of the storeroom door to make sure no one was within earshot. "You know how I sometimes say things that are a bit strange."

Charlie nodded. "Like com-put-ers . . . and . . . phones . . . and girls playing football?"

Sam nodded. "You see, I don't come from your time. I'm from the twenty-first century." Charlie's eyes grew wide with amazement and her mouth dropped open as he told her how the coin brought him to the *Sea Wolf*. "That's why I appeared from nowhere," he finished.

"You're talking like a mad man," said Charlie, waving the mop again.

Sam took out his coin. "I swear a pirate's oath on Silver's doubloon that I am a time traveller."

Charlie looked thoughtful.

"You know you can trust me," Sam insisted. "I helped you escape from your stepfather's men, didn't I?"

"Well, yes . . ." Charlie admitted.

"And I didn't tell the crew that you were really a girl, did I?"

"No."

"And when they found out and said females were bad luck on board," Sam went on, "I tried to stop them making you walk the plank."

"That's true," said Charlie slowly.

"Then you have to believe this," pleaded Sam. "But don't tell anyone, not even Fernando."

Charlie put down her mop. "Very well." She grinned. "Your secret's safe with me. The crew would think *I* was mad if I told them the tale you've just told me."

Sam held up his hand. "High five!" Charlie looked puzzled. "It's what we do in the future when we're happy. You slap my hand with yours."

Charlie smacked her palm onto his. "The men will be delighted to find that you're alive!" she exclaimed.

"There's only one problem," said Sam. "How am I going to explain where I've been?"

CHAPTER TWO

"Hey, everyone!" shouted Charlie, darting up the storeroom steps and onto the deck. "Come and see who's here!"

Sam followed her, shielding his eyes from the sudden bright sunlight. The *Sea Wolf* was speeding through the blue waves, her patched sails full of wind. It was great to be back.

"Well, run me up the flagpole!" gasped a

happy-looking pirate, dropping the barrel he was mending. "We thought you were dead, boy!"

"We did indeed, Ned," said Harry Hopp, the first mate. He snapped his spyglass shut and hurried over to shake Sam firmly by the hand, his peg leg clacking on the wooden boards. "Someone tell Captain Blade."

"I can see him with my own eyes!" A tall man in a tricorn hat and belts full of weapons strode across the deck. It was Captain Blade, the bold leader of the pirate band. "By Jupiter," he boomed, "we never thought to set eyes on our lookout boy again."

"We were sure you'd fallen from the crow's nest and drowned," Ned told him. "We only found your spyglass, jerkin, neckerchief and belt and we left them there as a mark of respect to a brave buccaneer."

"'Twas enough to make a grown man weep," added Peter the cook, wiping his eyes.

"But where have you been, lad?" demanded the captain. "You never asked permission to go ashore."

Sam gulped. What could he say?

"I can answer that," said Charlie quickly. "What does a pirate love most of all?"

Sam gawped at her. What was she doing? Everyone knew pirates loved treasure best. If they thought he'd gone off after gold they'd have him walking the plank before you could say shiver me timbers.

"That be easy for me," answered Harry Hopp. "It's my old mum."

"Aye," chorused the pirates. "Our mothers!"

"Well, that's where Sam was," said

Charlie, looking at him and nodding hard. "Weren't you, Sam?"

Sam got the message. "That's right," he said. "I had to go home and help my mum." That was true. Sam had been whisked back to the future without any warning. And just in time to help out on the till in his parents' fish and chip shop.

"Of course he'd put his mother first!" declared Harry Hopp. "He's a Silver. There be a noble heart beating inside this lad." He scratched his bald head. "One thing I can't fathom, Sam. How did you leave the ship without taking one of the rowing boats?"

"Well . . . erm . . ." sputtered Sam.

Charlie came to his rescue again. "He's a Silver!" she exclaimed. "He knows how to sneak about. You wouldn't ask him to give away all his pirate tricks, would you?"

There were more slaps on the back for Sam at this. Even Sinbad, the surly ship's cat, gave him a friendly hiss.

"You're a chip off the old block, Sam!" chuckled Ned. "Isn't he just like his old grandad?"

The crew had decided that Sam must be Joseph Silver's grandson. Sam couldn't tell them that it was sort of true, but that there were a lot of greats in between.

Swoosh! A knife flashed down past Sam's nose and landed on the deck between his feet. A skinny boy with wild curly hair was swinging from the rigging above his head.

Sam grinned and pulled the knife out of the boards. "I see you haven't lost your aim, Fernando!"

His friend jumped down on to the deck. "How do you know I wasn't aiming at you?" he said fiercely. He spoke with a strong Spanish accent. "You deserve it for leaving like that." Then he grinned and gave Sam a bear hug that nearly knocked the air out of him. "But I'm glad to see you."

"It's good to have you on board again, lad," said Captain Blade. "Especially as we've got a sniff of more treasure."

"Cool!" gasped Sam.

"Cool?" Ned put his huge hand on Sam's forehead. "Are you ill, boy?" he asked anxiously. "It's hotter than a baker's oven today!"

"I'm fine," said Sam quickly. He had to remember to be careful what he said. He didn't want the crew thinking he was mad.

"I mean, that's wonderful, Captain. Is the treasure on an island like before?"

"No, it's on a Spanish merchant ship this time," Captain Blade told him, a gleam in his eye. "She's carrying gold from South America for the Spanish King. But we've decided His Majesty has plenty already and that this shall be *Sea Wolf* booty."

"Excellent," said Sam. "We'll have loads more treasure to go with the loot we found on Skeleton Island."

Everyone fell silent. Several pirates began to blush and Sinbad suddenly became very interested in cleaning his ears.

"Ah," said Harry Hopp, shuffling his peg leg in embarrassment. "We don't have much of that left. To tell you the truth, our chests are empty. We bought lots of supplies with it, you see."

"And then we stood drinks for everyone in the tavern," added Ned. "Twice."

"And then we made a wager," admitted

Harry Hopp. "We bet the crew of the *Jolly Swordfish* that Peter could eat more pies than their own cook."

"I lost!" said Peter, patting his skinny belly mournfully. "And it had taken me all morning to cook those pies."

Sam tried not to laugh. Peter's cooking was so terrible that even the rats turned their noses up at it.

Captain Blade twisted his ring on his finger. Even he looked a bit embarrassed. "I'm sorry to say we borrowed your share of the gold, lad," he admitted. "We had to pay for Peter to see a doctor afterwards."

Sam looked round at the red-faced crew. "Don't worry about that," he said cheerfully. "I can't take it back to my mum, can I?" That was true. He couldn't take anything back to the future, but the crew were looking puzzled.

"He has to travel light," said Charlie quickly, giving Sam a glare.

"That's right," agreed Sam. "It's difficult to sneak about with pockets full of gold." He rubbed his hands together. "So you really need this Spanish booty then."

"That we do, lad," answered the captain. "And you're just in time to take over from Seth on lookout duty. Get up to that crow's nest — on the double!"

"Aye, aye, Captain," declared Sam, giving a smart salute. "I'll soon spy those scurvy Spaniards!"

CHAPTER THREE

Sam was halfway up the rigging for his lookout duty when he heard a deafening squawk above him. He jumped in surprise and nearly fell overboard. He looked up to see a flurry of bright green feathers, a hooked beak and a pair of beady black eyes. A parrot was perched on the edge of the crow's nest, staring solemnly down at him.

"Just what we need on the *Sea Wolf!*" exclaimed Sam in delight. "Every pirate ship should have a parrot." The parrot flew down onto Sam's shoulder and peered sideways at him. "Yo ho ho," it said solemnly.

"A pirate parrot!" said Sam. "Even better. Come and meet the captain." He scrambled down to the main deck, the parrot clinging to his shoulder.

Fernando was laying out a torn sail, his long, curly hair falling over his face.

"Ahoy, me hearty," squawked the parrot in greeting.

Fernando dropped his sail. "Where did

you get that?" he asked. To Sam's surprise he looked nervous.

"It was up in the crow's nest," said Sam. "What's the matter, Fernando? Don't you like parrots?"

"*I* like them all right," replied Fernando, giving the parrot a scratch under its chin. "But Captain Blade . . . well, that's a different matter. He won't have one on board. He's scared of them."

"Captain Blade?" said Sam in amazement. "But he's not scared of anything. He's the most fearless pirate in the Caribbean."

"Keep your voice down!" warned Fernando. "I heard that a parrot stole his rattle when he was a baby. He won't let one aboard the *Sea Wolf*."

"But every pirate ship has to have a parrot," protested Sam.

"Not this one," said Fernando. He glanced over Sam's shoulder. "Look, here he comes now. You'd better hide." He grinned wickedly. "Good luck!"

Sam ducked behind the biggest cannon on the deck, taking the parrot with him.

"Man the guns," the parrot said in his ear.

"Shhh!" hissed Sam. He heard Fernando stifling a chuckle.

Captain Blade strode by, his weapons glinting in his belt and his long hair blowing in the wind. "There's no one on lookout," he growled. "Where's Sam? Gone back to his mother again? I'll skin the boy if I find him."

Sam realised he was going to be in big trouble. He'd have to sneak up to the crow's nest without being seen – taking his new friend with him.

But the parrot had spied the captain. "Avast, you scurvy knave!" he squawked.

The captain whipped round. "Who said that?" he demanded.

Sam pushed the parrot under the cannon and jumped to his feet. "Just me, sir," he said. "Practising my best pirate talk."

"Barnacles on your bottom!" the parrot remarked from his hiding place.

"That wasn't you," the captain said, turning pale. "Your lips didn't move."

There was a loud flapping sound and the parrot flew out, perched on the captain's hat and began to eat the brim.

Sam could see Fernando laughing behind his sail.

Captain Blade froze. "Is that what I think it is?" he quavered.

Sam thought quickly. "Er, no. It's not a parrot," he said boldly. "It was in the crow's nest, so it must be a crow! I thought you'd like to meet the new crew member before I start my duty."

"A crow, you say?" whispered the captain, quaking in his boots. "It's a bit colourful for a crow, isn't it?"

"It's a Caribbean crow," said Sam firmly.

"But crows don't talk," said the captain.

"Caribbean crows do," insisted Sam.

"It's definitely a Caribbean crow," called Fernando.

"Crow!" shrieked the parrot.

"See," said Sam. "It even knows its name. Good bird, Crow."

He coaxed the parrot onto his finger.

Captain Blade straightened his nibbled

hat and set off for the wheel, looking white under his long beard. "That . . . crow had better keep out of my way or it'll be walking the plank," he growled. "And so will you if you don't get up on duty this instant, Sam Silver!"

Parrot on his shoulder, Sam shot up the rigging and pulled himself into the little basket near the top of the mast.

Crow hopped onto the rail. "Hoist the mizzen sail!" he squawked loudly. "Yo ho ho!"

"A word of advice," Sam warned him. "Don't yo ho ho near the captain if you want to be a *Sea Wolf* parrot."

He raised his spyglass and scanned the water for signs of the Spanish galleon. The sea sparkled in the bright sun and although there were a couple of ships in the distance, Sam could tell they were pirate vessels from their battered hulls and dark sails. Captain Blade wouldn't be wasting time fighting them today, not when he was on the trail of treasure.

Sam looked proudly down at his own ship. The leaping wolf figurehead jutted proudly from the bows and the snarling wolf-head and crossbones fluttered from the mainmast.

He raised his spyglass again. Far in the distance he saw a flash of white sail. He trained his spyglass on the mast to identify the flag.

"Ship ahoy, Captain!" he yelled. "Off the starboard bow. Three o'clock." Sam had learned to look at the sea as if it was a clock face and the ship was in the middle of it. Straight ahead was twelve o'clock and directly behind, over the stern, was six.

Captain Blade adjusted his spyglass. "White flag with Spanish coat of arms," he announced. "Three-decker and well armed. She's the *San Paulo*. That's our prey!"

He turned with excitement to his eager crew. "All hands on deck!" he bellowed. "Fire some shots across their bows to show we mean business. That treasure will soon be ours!"

Chapter Four

Sam's heart was pounding with excitement as he sped down the rigging. The *Sea Wolf* was coming alongside the *San Paulo*. Through the cannon smoke he could just see his crew lobbing ropes with grappling hooks at the enemy ship. They fastened like claws to the rigging. Now the Spanish vessel couldn't get away. Two pirates were beating a fierce rhythm on drums to spark fear into the Spaniards.

"Man the guns!" squawked Crow, flying down onto Sam's shoulder.

"You can't come with me," said Sam urgently. He put out a finger and the parrot hopped onto it. "Stay on this barrel till I get back. You'll be safe here."

Miaow! A ball of black fur shot out of nowhere and threw itself at the barrel. "Abandon ship!" screeched Crow, flapping back up to the top of the mast in a panic.

Sinbad sat himself on the barrel, his yellow eyes fixed on the parrot. *Whoops!* thought Sam. He'd forgotten about the ship's cat.

"Sorry, Crow," he called. "But you'll be even safer up there!"

"Forward!" commanded Blade. At his command the pirates began to scramble along the ropes with bloodthirsty yells.

Captain Blade swung across to land on the deck of the *San Paulo*. Sam followed.

"Right behind you!" cried Charlie.

"Me too!" yelled Fernando.

The three friends landed squarely on the enemy deck. More of the *Sea Wolf*'s crew poured across to join them, jumping over the rail, cutlasses at the ready. Sam prepared for attack – but the ship looked deserted.

"There's no one here," whispered Charlie, gripping her cutlass hard.

"Then they be hiding," growled the first mate, stamping his peg leg. "'Tis strange though. I didn't think the Spanish soldiers would be so lily-livered."

"Show yourselves, you cowards!"

shouted the captain, raising his sword.

One by one, the enemy crew crept out from behind barrels and cannon. Sam had a good look at them. He'd expected to see shiny breastplates and helmets but these men were in white vests and short breeches. Surely the King of Spain sent armed guards with his treasure, yet there wasn't a weapon or a piece of armour in sight.

Wow! thought Sam. *That must be the quickest surrender in the history of piracy.* He'd certainly made the enemy quake in their boots – well, him and a few others!

One of the Spanish sailors, pale and gibbering, called something in his own language.

"You speak their lingo, Fernando," said the captain. "What's he telling us?"

"He says we'll find nothing here," Fernando translated. "He claims their cargo has already been taken. But I think he's hiding something, Captain." He flashed his knife at the quivering enemy.

"Tell them that if this is a trap they'll all pay the price," said Captain Blade sternly.

Fernando rapped out a string of angry Spanish. Sam guessed from the horrified expressions on the faces of the listeners that he was threatening them with the worst fate imaginable. He smiled to himself. The most Captain Blade would ever do was set them adrift in their own rowing boat. He was too honourable to put even his worst enemy to death! But the Spaniards didn't know that.

"And if this is a trap," the captain went on, "we will soon spring it. We'll keep these snivelling dogs on deck. Harry, Ned, take some men and go below to look for that treasure. Sam, you go too. If anyone can uncover trickery, it's a Silver."

"Aye, aye, Captain." Cutlass drawn, Sam followed the men down to the lower decks.

"Split up," ordered the first mate.

"Shout if you find anything."

Sam came to a gun deck. There was no sign of enemy sailors or guards. The cannon stood in endless rows, black and shiny. But something was wrong. He realised that there wasn't a cannonball or powder keg in sight. After checking every corner he made for the long ladder that led down to the hold, deep in the bowels of the ship. It was pitch black down there. Sam took the lantern that swung above his head and crept down the steps, eyes darting everywhere, ears straining for sounds of movement. The shadows danced in the flickering lantern flame.

He made his way cautiously around the hold, ready for any attack. Even in this huge store area

there was no sign of weapons, food, or even water. There were just a few empty boxes and barrels. Nothing that could hold the treasure which was meant to be on board. Sam was about to go back up on deck and report, when a low moan echoed round in the darkness.

The sound was hardly human. Was someone trying to frighten him? Well, they weren't going to manage that! Sam Silver had his cutlass at the ready.

He heard the groan again. It was coming from the far corner of the hold. Sam crept slowly towards the sound. With a wild cry, a figure suddenly lurched out of the dark. Sam jumped back, his sword raised, but the man just grovelled on the floor, whimpering. Sam could see lines of real fear on his face.

"I won't hurt you," he said, putting up his sword. He pointed to the ladder and the man stumbled up to the deck where

he fell to his knees in front of Captain
Blade. Fernando glared suspiciously at the
newcomer and fingered his knife.

Harry and Ned had already returned.

"The ship's empty," Sam reported. "No
food, no ammunition – and no treasure."

"Aye," agreed Harry. "We found
nothing either."

The sailor from the hold called
something in Spanish to his shipmates.
Eyes full of terror, they nodded. He

looked up at Captain Blade and began to speak in a low, trembling voice. Fernando didn't translate immediately. Instead he listened intently and his eyes grew wide with fear.

"What's he saying?" demanded the captain. "Tell us, lad."

Fernando turned to face the *Sea Wolf* crew. "He's saying that the *San Paulo* was attacked and everything was taken by a vessel that came out of a wall of fog . . ." He gulped. "And it was no ordinary vessel. It was a *ghost ship!*"

Chapter Five

A shiver ran through the crew of the *Sea Wolf*.

"I believe he's telling the truth," said Captain Blade. "No one could act such terror."

"I remember tales of a ghost ship," muttered Harry Hopp, anxiously rubbing his stubbly chin. "She was called the *Queen Caterina*. A cursed vessel

 if ever there was one."

Some of the older pirates nodded.

"Tell me about it," said Sam. He loved ghost stories – they made his spine tingle as if icy fingers were running up and down it.

"I was told the story when I was a child," explained Captain Blade. "The *Queen Caterina* was a Spanish galleon. She was attacked and sunk by pirates a century ago."

Harry Hopp nodded. "'Twas said that there was no hope for any on board and, as the captain drowned, he cried out that the seas had not seen the last of the doomed ship. She'd rise again from Davy Jones' Locker and wreak her revenge on all who sailed the oceans. Any man who laid eyes on her would perish."

"Wow!" breathed Sam. "What happened next?"

Harry lowered his voice to a whisper. "Soon after, the broken old galleon rose again from the ocean floor. She appeared to sailors, glowing in the dark and crewed by a ghastly band of ghouls!"

Sam felt a fizz of fear and excitement all mixed together. It was like being on the ghost train at the fair. He was always the first into the carriage – and the one who yelled the loudest at the sight of the spooks.

"But I never heard they plundered treasure in them days," murmured Ned, wide-eyed. "They just put a curse on folk and scared 'em to death." He gestured towards the cowering Spanish crew. "That's why this lot think they're done for."

"I'd wager the *Queen Caterina*'s still around these waters," said Harry. He slapped his wooden leg. "Stap me, I feel it in my missing bones — and they never lie."

"We must get back and protect the *Sea Wolf*," declared Ned.

Captain Blade slid his cutlass back in his belt. "Aye, everyone return to the ship." He caught Ben the quartermaster by the arm. "Find these poor wretches some food before we sail . . . as long as Peter hasn't had his hands on it. They've suffered enough already."

"Aye, aye, Captain." Sam grabbed the rail, ready to jump back to their ship. But he stopped as his hand touched something strange and sticky.

He looked down at his palm. It was covered in a sort of gloopy goo. He wiped it on the rail but it wouldn't come off his hand. He'd never seen anything like it on the *Sea Wolf*. He gave it a sniff and wished he hadn't. It smelt like rotting fish.

"What's this?" he asked the nearest Spaniard, showing him his hand.

The man backed away, his eyes wide with terror. "*Fantasma!*" he croaked, making the sign of the cross on his chest.

Sam had heard the word *fantasma* when Fernando was translating for the captain. He'd bet all the treasure in the world that it meant "ghost" in Spanish. So the man was saying that a ghost had left the strange stuff behind. He'd seen something like that in *Ghostgrabbers* on the telly. The presenter had said ghosts left spooky gloop behind all the time. And now he was seeing it for real!

Sam grabbed a rope and swung back to

his ship. He quickly found Charlie and stuck his hand under her nose.

"I've got ghostly goo on me," he said.

Charlie gasped. "It smells worse than Hell itself. You may be cursed too!"

"Don't be daft," said Sam. "It'd take more than a bit of ghostly goo to curse me."

Charlie still looked worried. "That's because you're from the future. We see things differently. The crew will be very frightened by this. I don't think you should tell anyone else, not even Fernando."

"My lips are sealed," said Sam. He gave Charlie a wicked grin. "You know, if I went back home now with this stuff on my hands, they'd be interviewing me on the telly."

"Shhh!" said Charlie. "I don't know what you're babbling on about but don't say that sort of thing to anyone else either." She grabbed his arm. "You're not going back now, are you?"

"No way!" declared Sam. "Well, not if I can help it. The coin decides, not me." He noticed that Captain Blade and Harry Hopp were by the wheel, studying a map. "Wonder where we're off to now. I'm going to find out."

As he went across the deck towards them he heard a *miaow* above his head. Sinbad was sitting on one of the yards that held the sails in place, licking his lips smugly. Sam felt a sudden pang of alarm. He'd forgotten all about his new feathered shipmate. Had Sinbad just enjoyed a Crow dinner?

"Repel all boarders!" came a chirpy squawk. To Sam's relief the green parrot was on top of the mast. He seemed perfectly happy, preening his bright plumage and ignoring the cat below.

Phew! thought Sam. It seemed that Crow could look after himself.

"We'll be needing to look elsewhere for

treasure," the first mate was saying as Sam joined them.

"I've been thinking," answered Captain Blade. "If the *Queen Caterina* is sailing these waters, I've a mind to find her."

"That would be great, Captain!" exclaimed Sam. He really wanted to see this ship with its phantom crew. It would be better – and scarier – than any TV programme or film. "The crew are frightened of ghosts, though, aren't they, sir?"

Captain Blade gave a huge guffaw. "But I am not and they'll follow me, Sam! I'll face a hundred phantoms if it means we can get our hands on that Spanish gold. I've not heard of any other treasure hoard in this area so that's the one we're after. Look lively, men!" he shouted. "We've got a ghost ship to find!"

Some of the crew stopped and stared at him in horror.

"Do we want to end up like those poor gibbering Spaniards?" asked Ben faintly.

"Belay that talk, Ben Hudson," declared Harry Hopp. "We're *Sea Wolf* pirates. We don't scare easy."

The crew turned back to their duties but Sam noticed that they gave each other worried looks.

"What course do I steer, Captain?" asked Harry, taking the wheel.

Captain Blade looked at the map again. "The Spaniards were coming from Nombre de Dios in Panama." He prodded

the map with his finger. "Looking at their route, I'd wager that this is where the cursed *Caterina* will be hiding."

"I don't understand," said Sam, staring at the parchment. "There's nothing marked there, just sea. There's nowhere for a ship to hide."

"Aye, it seems like that on the chart," said Blade. "But there's something there that no map will show."

"I think I know what you mean," gasped Sam. "The Spanish said the ship came out of a wall of fog."

"That's it, lad." Captain Blade's eyes flashed with excitement. "But we know it as the Cloud of Death!"

CHAPTER SIX

Sam saw Harry Hopp turn pale. Charlie and Fernando exchanged anxious looks.

"The Cloud of Death is a strange bank of fog," explained the captain. "No matter what the weather, it hangs heavy over that stretch of the ocean. You sail blind if you go in there and it hides many a sharp rock. We always set a course around it."

Harry nodded. "Aye, or be wrecked. That place is surely cursed."

Sam heard the pirates begin to whisper. A nearby seaman pushed Ben forwards.

"Excuse me, Captain," he said nervously. "Me and the crew are not sure we want to go anywhere near the Cloud of Death."

Captain Blade's fierce gaze swept over them.

"Call yourselves buccaneers?" he boomed. "We sail under the *Sea Wolf* flag and we are scared of nothing!"

Sam wasn't sure this was quite true. Captain Blade might fear nothing – apart from parrots – but his crew looked as if they'd rather sit in a shark-infested bath than face a shipload of ghosts.

The captain strode up and down the deck, glaring at his gibbering men. "We've fought Blackheart and his men, and we've always lived to tell the tale."

"Aye," nodded Harry Hopp. "We're a brave crew."

"But what about the curse?" quavered Ben.

"I don't want to die!" said Peter the cook.

"We risk death every time we eat your seaweed stew!" muttered Ned. He stepped up to Blade's side. "I'm with the captain. If he thinks we can get that gold, then we should make the attempt."

"Spoken like a true pirate, Ned!" exclaimed Blade. "We'll have no lily-livered cowards on the *Sea Wolf*."

"Count me in!" said Charlie.

"And me!" added Fernando.

"But it's a ship full of phantoms," came a voice from the back. "Our cutlasses will go straight through them."

"And *their* cutlasses will not harm us in return," said the captain firmly. There were mutterings of agreement at that.

Blade grinned and his eyes flashed. "Think on it. The *Queen Caterina*'s gold is ours for the taking – there'll be no other ships brave enough to venture near the place."Sam could see the men's eyes brightening and their backs straightening as they thought about this.

"If we turn back now, we'll be a bunch of yellow-bellied poltroons!" cried the captain. "But I know you to be a brave crew who would fight the Devil himself if I asked!"

Now the men were standing tall, eyes fixed on the captain.

Blade raised his cutlass above his head. "Are you with me, men?" he shouted.

"Aye!" cried the crew as one.

"Then steer a course for the Cloud of Death, my brave band," ordered Blade. "South south-west. Sam, get up on lookout and alert us the second you spy that infernal bank of fog."

Sam sped up the rigging and into the crow's nest.

"Ahoy there!" squawked the parrot, hopping onto his shoulder and squawking a loud sea shanty in his ear.

"Thanks, Crow," shouted Sam above the deafening racket. "I'm glad to see you've stayed out of Sinbad's way, but keep your beak shut. I've got to concentrate. We're off to find a ghost ship." The parrot peered at him, head on one side. "It's going to be brilliant. Like *Ghostgrabbers* on the telly."

"On the telly," repeated the parrot.

"Whoops," said Sam. "I'd better be careful what I say in front of you."

He grabbed hold of the rail as the ship lurched suddenly. The waves were higher now and the *Sea Wolf* was rising with them. Far ahead the sky was full of black clouds. Lightning zigzagged and driving rain streaked the darkening sky.

"Batten down the hatches!" shrieked Crow, flapping to the floor of the lookout basket.

Sam put his hands to his mouth and yelled to the captain, "Storm dead ahead!"

Curtains of rain swept over the *Sea Wolf*. The sky was murky grey, but every now and again it was lit with brilliant flashes of jagged lightning, quickly followed by deafening cracks of thunder. Sam could see sailors down below tying safety lines along the deck so that they could cling to them as the sea tossed the ship about. Spray blew in his face, blurring his vision. Towering waves were coming at them relentlessly. The *Sea Wolf* faced each one head on. No sooner had the ship reached a peak than she plunged into a dark trough.

"Abandon ship!" screeched Crow. He flapped into the air in panic, nearly got blown away and dived down again to cling to Sam's legs. Sam shook his wet hair out

of his eyes. His job was more important
than ever now. He had to make sure the
ship wasn't thrown on to rocks – but
how? He could hardly see anything in the
blinding downpour and they hadn't even
found the Cloud of Death yet!

A shudder ran through the *Sea Wolf*. "A
plank's given way on the hull," came a yell
from below. "We're shipping water."

Through the rain Sam saw Fernando
and some of the crew hanging on to the
safety ropes as they made for the hold to
man the pumps. His stomach gave a jolt.
Were they going to sink? They needed to
find land – and quickly!

He turned a circle on his lookout post,
Crow clinging to his jeans like a limpet.
Nothing but storm-tossed seas. But what
was that? Another ship? He wiped the
water from his spyglass lens and looked
again. No it couldn't be. It wasn't moving
and he could make out waves crashing on

to a stretch of beach. It was an island! If they could reach it they might just be safe.

"Land ahoy!" he bellowed through the noise of the storm. "To starboard. Two o'clock."

Captain Blade barked orders to the men. The sailors formed lines and heaved on the sail ropes.

The ship swung slowly until the bow was aiming at the small patch of land. But now the waves were striking her amidships, tipping her from side to side. Water sloshed over the deck to run away through the rails. High above, Sam could do nothing but hang on for his life against the violent rocking. *It's like a rollercoaster ride*, he thought to himself as the crow's nest dipped towards the waves, then swooshed back up again.

Except this ride could be deadly!

Suddenly the biggest wave Sam had ever seen was looming over them. The *Sea Wolf*

tilted dangerously as she was swept up
by the surging water. Sam's feet slipped
from under him. He flung out his arms
and grasped the rail. But now the ship was
almost on her side and he found himself
flung out of the crow's nest. He hung by
his fingers over the raging sea, with Crow
clinging to his ankle and flapping his
wings in terror. Sam's arms felt as if they
were being pulled out of their sockets. His
fingers were losing their grip. He couldn't
hold on much longer.

CHAPTER SEVEN

All Sam could see below him was the churning sea. He tensed his knuckles, desperate to hold on. The *Sea Wolf* reached the crest of the wave. She lurched and swung violently upright. Sam had to let go. He was somersaulted into the air and felt himself falling. Any second now he'd be swallowed up by the violent waves. He collided with something hard. The mast had

saved him. He tumbled in a heap into the
crow's nest. He struggled to his feet, Crow
still clinging to his leg, and looked out. Sam
couldn't believe his eyes. The *Sea Wolf* was
surfing the wave towards the island!

The ruffled parrot climbed up his
trousers, onto his shoulder and peered into
his face. "Shark bait?" he enquired.

"We very nearly were!" agreed Sam.

A sudden burst of light in the clouds
had him bracing himself, waiting for the
next crash of thunder. But it didn't come.

Sam realised it wasn't lightning. It was a tiny glimmer of blue sky. The clouds were breaking up. Beams of bright sunlight began to filter through the grey. The huge wave gradually sank until it died away to a gentle swell and the rain stopped. They'd weathered the storm.

The *Sea Wolf* dropped anchor in the calm waters off the little island.

Sam scrambled down the rigging and high fived with Charlie. Fernando looked at them, puzzled.

"What's this?" he asked. "Is it some strange dance where you come from, Sam?"

"It means we're happy," said Sam, holding up his hand. "High five, Fernando!"

Fernando whacked Sam's hand as hard as he could.

"That's it," croaked Sam, cradling his

stinging palm. "But don't break my fingers next time."

Harry Hopp had just finished a head count.

"All present and accounted for, Captain," he announced with a grin.

"You did handsomely spotting this island, Sam," said Captain Blade. "Mr Hopp, take a landing party to fell timber for repairs. The rest keep the water out as best you can till they get back. There'll be a tot of rum for everyone when the work's done. You all deserve it."

Sam groaned inwardly. He couldn't think why pirates loved their rum so much — one sip of it and he felt as if his tongue had caught fire and steam was coming out of his ears.

Harry took a rowing boat and set off at once with a willing band of men.

Sam surveyed the shore. There was hardly any land to be seen, just rocks leading up a hill to a dense forest.

"There'll be good fresh fruit here, I reckon," said Fernando, joining him at the ship's rail.

"And fresh water for our barrels," added Charlie.

"Then let's explore!" declared Sam, a mischievous glint in his eye. "Permission to go ashore, Captain?"

They rowed the second boat to the water's edge and stood on the rocks, looking back at the *Sea Wolf* with its ragged hole on the waterline. Their wet clothes began to steam in the hot sunshine.

"It was lucky you saw land, my friend," said Fernando, as they set off towards the forest. "I was on bailing duty in the hold when the waves hit us. The water was rising faster than we could pump."

"Happy to be of service," said Sam with a bow.

They made their way through waving palm trees, pushing through dense, dark vegetation and tangles of vine that caught at their feet. As they climbed the hill, animal and bird cries echoed strangely from the forest canopy.

"This is amazing!" breathed Sam, gazing at a massive centipede crawling up a tree trunk. It was longer than his forearm.

There was a deafening shriek and something landed on him. "Help!" he yelled. "I'm being attacked!"

"Avast, yer landlubber!" came a squawk in his ear.

Sam looked round to see Crow's beady

eye staring into his. Charlie and Fernando collapsed with laughter.

The parrot made himself comfortable on Sam's shoulder. "Yo ho ho," he screeched, giving Sam a friendly nibble. "All present and correct!"

They marched on uphill, picking guavas and the little brown fruits that Fernando called mammee apples. They ate some and stashed the rest in sacks. They hadn't gone far when the land suddenly began to slope downwards.

"This is a very small island," said Fernando. "We'll be at the other side before you can say Hispaniola."

"You're right," said Sam. "There's the sea again."

"What's that?" gasped Charlie, clutching at the boys' sleeves to stop them going any further. "Down by the water's edge."

They ducked and Sam parted the leaves in front of him. He peered out at a fence

of tree trunks which circled a rough
building inside.

"It's a hut of some kind, with a stockade
round it," he told them.

"We must be careful," said Fernando,
his hand on the hilt of his knife. "There
could be people here and they may not be
friendly – especially to pirates."

"Then we'll check it out and tell the
captain," said Sam.

"And we have to do it secretly," added
Charlie. "The captain wants his crew in
one piece."

"One piece!" squawked the parrot cheerfully.

"It's difficult to be secret with Crow here," groaned Sam.

Fernando tossed a mammee apple onto the ground. Crow pounced on it with a whistle of delight. "That'll keep him quiet."

Leaving Crow to enjoy his snack, they crept forwards until they found themselves close to the hut. It was a rough building with holes hewn out for windows and a doorway. The trees had been cut down to make a clearing that led to the water's edge.

"Can't hear anything," whispered Sam as they hid behind a boulder.

"That doesn't mean there's no one there," replied Charlie, her eyes darting nervously about.

Fernando peered round the boulder, checking out the lie of the land. "Let's split up," he hissed. "I'll take the door,

you two take the windows. Make sure
you're not seen."

Together they ran silently across the
clearing. As they tiptoed round the
stockade they came to a huge gaping hole
where the fencing was smashed. They
crept through and darted over to the hut.
Sam inched up and peeped in through the
window on his side.

The single room was small, with a rough
earth floor and deep shadowy corners.

"All safe," called Fernando from the
doorway. "There's no one here. I wonder
who it belongs to."

"Let's search for clues," said Sam.

The three friends tiptoed inside, peering into empty sacks and turning over broken crates.

"This has the mark of a pirate hideout," said Fernando thoughtfully. "It's a good store for booty."

"But look at the mess," said Sam. "They're either very untidy pirates or it's been plundered. That fence was damaged on purpose and this place has been cleared in a hurry. Do you think another band of pirates attacked it?"

"Looks like it," muttered Charlie.

"We should get back to the *Sea Wolf* to report," said Fernando.

Sam had reached the door when he felt something stick to the bottom of his trainer. He lifted his foot.

It was the same strange gloopy stuff that he'd found on the Spanish ship. And he could smell rotting fish again. He looked up to see a trail of goo leading down to the jetty. He knew Charlie had told him to say nothing about the phantom substance but this was an important clue. He decided to point it out without telling Fernando he'd already got some on his skin. He didn't want his friend to think he'd been cursed.

"Wait," he said, showing them the trail. "There was some of this on the *San Paulo* and one of the Spaniards said it had come from the ghosts – the *fantasma*."

Fernando's eyes widened with fear.

"Are you saying it was the ghost crew that plundered this place?" asked Charlie in a tiny voice.

"It must have been," said Sam, gulping as a thought suddenly struck him. "They could be here, watching us even now."

"Watching!" came an eerie voice that echoed round the hut.

"Run!" shouted Fernando.

Sam and Charlie didn't need telling twice. They turned and followed Fernando in a mad dash through the forest towards the *Sea Wolf*. Behind them they could hear a low muttering voice and the distant rustling of leaves.

Something was following!

CHAPTER EIGHT

The three friends burst on to the rocky shore and collapsed, gasping for breath.

"What was that?" panted Charlie.

"One of the phantom crew for sure," said Fernando. "I caught a flash of ghostly green. It was terrible."

"I think I know what it was," said Sam, struggling to keep his face straight. "Did it have scaly claws?"

"Probably," said Fernando, turning pale.

"And did it have black eyes that bored into your very soul?" Sam asked in a sinister whisper.

"I didn't look," croaked Charlie. "But it said it was watching."

"Then you'd better *watch* out!" Sam leapt to his feet and pointed to the trees. "It's coming!"

Fernando and Charlie cowered, their hands over their heads. There was a flurry of feathers and Crow shot out of the forest. "Watching!" he squawked, circling round them. "Watching!"

Sam held his sides and laughed helplessly. Fernando grabbed him round the legs and pulled him over, shoving a handful of sand down his shirt.

"Good one, Crow," chuckled Charlie as the parrot landed on Sam's stomach. "But why did he follow us like that?"

"Probably making sure he wasn't left behind," said Sam, giving Crow's feathers a ruffle.

They could see the crew having a rest further along the shore.

"Come on," said Fernando. "We must tell Captain Blade about the hut."

The captain was holding out the rum bottle as they ran up.

"No time for that, Captain," said Sam, glad to avoid the ghastly drink. "We've found a pirate hideout."

"Any gold?" asked Harry Hopp, eagerly rubbing his hands.

"No, it had been raided," answered Charlie, "by the phantom crew!"

There was a gasp from the pirates.

"How do you know it was the ghosts?" demanded Blade.

Sam told him about the strange substance he'd found.

"Then this is even better than we thought," said Blade happily. "The ghost ship must be packed to the gunwales with booty by now."

Sam was beginning to get used to the way the pirates spoke. He knew that the gunwales, or "gunnels" as the pirates pronounced it, were the tops of the ship's sides — and that meant that the *Queen Caterina* would be bursting with gold!

Most of the men cheered but one or two shook their heads. Blade drew himself up to his full height and glared at them. "And I say that booty is *Sea Wolf* treasure. Prepare to set sail for the Cloud of Death!" he commanded, his eyes boring into them. "And those whose knees are knocking can leave this crew now! Anyone wish to stay ashore?"

"Nay!" roared the crew.

"All aboard!" shrieked Crow, flapping his wings.

Captain Blade stopped. "Not him," he said, jerking a thumb at the parrot. "Leave him here, Sam. It's a good island for . . . crows."

Sam sat gloomily at the bows, practising his knots as the *Sea Wolf* ploughed on towards the Cloud of Death with Seth on lookout duty in the crow's nest. Harry Hopp had taught Sam a round turn and two half hitches. He'd told him that he could use the knot to tether himself to the mast if they had another storm. Sam was keeping himself busy but his heart wasn't in it, not since they'd left Crow on the island. He hoped his parrot was all right. He'd hated saying goodbye to him but he couldn't disobey the captain, so he'd piled

up mammee apples and crept away while
Crow was tucking in unsuspectingly. The
island was far behind them now as they
sailed south-west. Sam squinted in the late
afternoon sun. The sea was empty, not a sail
or a patch of land to be seen. Things just
wouldn't be the same without his cheeky
friend aboard.

"Ahoy there, me hearty!"

There was a flurry of wings and Crow
suddenly landed on his shoulder.

Sam couldn't believe his eyes. "You're
back," he gasped, stroking his friend's
feathered head. "Awesome!" Then he
remembered the captain's orders. He looked
round anxiously to make sure that Captain

Blade was nowhere near. "Just stay out of sight or he'll have us scrubbing the decks."

"Walk the plank?" asked the parrot.

"I hope not," said Sam. He scanned the horizon again. "I can't wait to see the Cloud of Death," he said. "We get sea mists at Backwater Bay and you can't see your hand in front of your face. Maybe it's like that. Or maybe it's like those cotton-wool clouds you get when you're up in a plane."

"In a plane!" shrieked the parrot, nibbling his ear.

"Shhh," warned Sam. "Keep your squawks down."

He looked out over the *Sea Wolf* figurehead as the ship cut through the waves. Far ahead something caught his attention. He dropped the rope and grabbed his spyglass. At first he thought he was seeing land – low white cliffs. But that couldn't be right. He'd seen on the map that there were no islands in this part of the Caribbean. Then he realised that it was moving, swirling slowly above the surface of the sea. Now he knew exactly what it was.

"Cloud of Death, ahoy!" yelled Seth from the crow's nest.

Captain Blade burst out of his cabin. "Hold the course, men," he yelled. "We're going straight in."

Sam quickly hid Crow in the storeroom and shut the door. He'd just have to keep him hidden from the captain. He ran back to the bows again, his heart thumping with excitement.

The fog bank loomed ahead, taller than the ship, the vapour at its edges moving like shadowy figures.

"That's so creepy!" breathed Sam.

"Fernando, Charlie!" Blade ordered. "Join Sam at the bows. We'll need all the young eyes we can muster once we enter the Cloud."

"Aye, aye," called Sam's friends.

The *Sea Wolf* left the bright sunlight

and entered the fog. At once they were surrounded by an eerie quiet. The only sounds that Sam could hear were the creaking of the ship's timbers and the water lapping against the hull. The tops of the masts disappeared into the dense grey swirls.

The sea was strangely calm. With no wind, the sails hung loose from the yards. Yet the *Sea Wolf* was not slowing.

"I warrant there be underwater currents here," muttered Harry Hopp.

"Or ghostly swimmers moving us

along," someone answered him.

"Belay that talk!" called Captain Blade. "All eyes on the water. We don't want to spring a leak from some hidden rock."

The crew clustered at the rails.

Wisps of fog brushed Sam's face like icy wet fingers. It was much colder here in the Cloud and his skin was covered in goose pimples. He rubbed his arms as he peered through the murky air. When he looked back towards the stern he couldn't see past the foredeck. It was as if the rest of the ship had vanished. The figures of the crew moved in and out of view looking like ghosts themselves.

"It's not hard to believe that phantoms live here," whispered Fernando, wiping his damp brow as he studied the water to starboard.

"It reminds me of a tale my nursemaid told," said Charlie in a low voice. "She swore that when there was fog over the graveyard, all the dead would walk!"

"I thought I heard a ghost in a graveyard once," said Sam. "It turned out to be a mobile ringing!"

Fernando stared hard at him.

"I mean . . . my bell ringing . . ." spluttered Sam. "I always keep one in my pocket in case I get lost."

Fernando looked at him pityingly. "I don't know what you're talking about, my friend. The fog's muddling your wits."

Charlie suddenly gave a cry and pointed at the water where a dark shadow was looming. "Rocks ahead! Off the port bow."

Sam heard the creak of the wheel spinning as Captain Blade changed course and the *Sea Wolf* slid past the rocks with barely a rope's width to spare.

"What heading are we on now?" asked Harry Hopp. "'Tis hard to tell with no sky to see."

"Davy Jones' Locker will be our destination," came Peter's cry from somewhere on the foggy deck.

"More rocks to starboard!" yelled Fernando as the jagged points appeared over the bow.

There was a ghastly scraping sound from the hull and the *Sea Wolf* shuddered to a halt. The fog closed in on them.

Then suddenly the thick vapour parted to reveal a long black bowsprit that seemed to hang in the air above.

"It's the ghost ship!" shrieked Charlie.

Everyone gazed in horror at the sight. The fog billowed and parted and now they

could see a broken hull lying on the rock,
smashed and rotten. A faded nameplate
hung by a couple of nails from its bows.

"By Jove," Captain Blade's voice rang
out from the wheel. "That's no ghost ship.
That's the *Falmouth*. It disappeared six
years ago and was never heard of again."

"So this was its fate," breathed Harry
Hopp. "And it looks like all hands lost,
God rest 'em."

"Is this the work of the ghosts?" breathed Ned.

"It is not," the captain bellowed through the fog. "It's the currents and rocks that did for them and I will not have the same happen to the *Sea Wolf*. Reverse course! Use the oars. We're going to leave the Cloud of Death."

Sam knew that the captain was right. There was too much danger here for the *Sea Wolf*, but his heart sank. It looked as if the adventure was over.

CHAPTER NINE

The *Sea Wolf* slid out of the fog into the late evening sunshine, propelled by the oars. Blade stared long and hard at the Cloud of Death.

"Are we giving up, Captain?" Sam heard Harry Hopp ask.

"Never!" Blade thumped his fist on the rail. "We need that treasure. But I can't fathom a safe way to go into the Cloud without sinking the ship." He stroked his beard thoughtfully. "There must be an answer. . ."

Sam gave a whoop of joy. They weren't giving up! They just needed a plan and he was determined to think of one.

At suppertime he sat with Fernando and Charlie in the storeroom. They had a plate of salt pork and ship's biscuits.

Crow was perched next to them, eyeing the food hopefully.

"I'm glad Crow came back," said Charlie, stroking his head.

"You'll never manage to keep that parrot hidden, Sam," protested Fernando. "Captain Blade is bound to find him."

"I'll just have to keep him out of the captain's way," declared Sam, tapping his biscuit to get rid of the weevils. "Anyway, listen, I've had an idea about how we can get to the ghost ship. We swim there with lanterns on our heads."

"That won't work," said Charlie, through a mouthful of meat. "We'd sink under the weight of the treasure on the way back."

"And you'd sink anyway, Charlie," said Fernando with a grin. "You can't swim."

"Then we disguise ourselves as a rich Spanish ship," suggested Sam. "That should bring them out of the fog fast enough."

"There's only one problem with that idea," said Fernando, feeding some crumbs to Crow. "We have no Spanish flag."

"Or uniforms," Charlie reminded him. "Or the right sails."

Merow!

Sinbad appeared from nowhere and launched himself at the parrot. The outstretched claws just missed Crow who flew up onto Charlie's head.

"Naughty puss!" said Charlie, wagging a finger at him.

Sinbad nuzzled against her, stretched and strolled off.

"I don't know how you have made friends with that fiend from hell," said Fernando in admiration. "He won't let the rest of us near him."

Sam watched as the cat squeezed through the tiniest of gaps between two crates, using his whiskers to make sure it was wide enough.

An idea bounced into his brain.

"I've got it!" he yelled.

Fernando laughed. "What mad notion have you got now? More bells ringing in your pocket?"

"This one's not mad," insisted Sam, leaping up and running out onto the deck.

It was dark now and the lanterns were lit. "Captain Blade, I think I have a plan for how we can get to the ghost ship."

"Then, by the stars, I want to hear it!" exclaimed Blade.

"It came from Sinbad," said Sam.

"Well, I'll eat a bowlful of barnacles!" said Ned. "Are you telling us that cat can speak?"

"No," said Sam with a grin. "I was watching him — from a safe distance, of course — and that's when I got the idea. We take a rowing boat and we hold out pikes in front to act like Sinbad's whiskers. The pikes will hit the rocks and we'll be able to steer clear of them even if we can't see them."

"It might work, Captain," said Fernando eagerly. "And a rowing boat would have a much shallower keel."

"Indeed," declared the captain, slapping Sam on the back. "It's an excellent plan, and worthy of your grandfather. We'll take both boats. There'll be room for more men – and more booty."

Quickly the captain sorted out two parties for the boats that were being lowered into the water. "Ned will take charge of one and I'll take the other. Fernando, Sam, you're with me. And bring Charlie. The three of you will only take the place of two men – and you can hold the pikes."

The boats were lashed one behind the other while the crew fetched pikes and took their seats. The captain sat at the tiller of the leading boat and called up to the first mate. "You're in command until we get back, Mr Hopp."

"Aye, aye, Captain."

"Yo ho ho!" To Sam's horror, Crow suddenly landed on his head.

The captain turned pale. "I thought we'd left that bird behind," he growled. "Did you disobey my orders, Sam Silver?"

"I'm sorry, Captain, but he found his way back on his own," blustered Sam. The parrot hopped down and dug his claws into his shoulder. "Ouch! He's got a bit attached to me, but he won't be any trouble."

"Trouble!" squawked Crow.

"Make sure he keeps to that," growled the captain. "We'll get rid of him at the next port. And that's my final word."

The fog closed about them and at once they felt the chill air touching their skin again. They edged along. It was darker now that night had fallen. Each boat had lanterns at the bow and stern to light the way. The three friends held their pikes out in front. Charlie pushed the end of hers under the water and moved it about, searching for rocks below the surface.

Sam shifted his grip on the heavy pike and saw that his palm was glowing green in the darkness. It was the ghostly goo! Somehow it was shining all on its own. He covered it up quickly, but not before Charlie had given a muffled gasp.

"Don't say anything to the others," she whispered in his ear.

Sam nodded but he could see she was biting her lip and kept glancing over at him.

Crunch!

Fernando tensed as his pike struck something solid.

"Pull to starboard," called the captain.

The oarsmen changed course and the boats glided safely past.

Sam's pike shuddered in his hands. "Rock, straight ahead!" he cried. A jagged peak loomed up out of the fog.

"Reverse oars," called the captain. He gave a low chuckle. "Your plan's going to be the saving of us, Sam. We'll reach that treasure yet." He moved the tiller. "Forward again, men."

"Hold hard," came Ned's voice. "I heard a sound."

The rowers stilled their oars and everyone listened. Sam could see Charlie's wide eyes in the lantern light.

They all heard the sound now. It was the creak of heavy timbers.

"It's a ship," warned Fernando.

"Slow ahead," said the captain in a low voice.

As the boats moved forwards the fog swirled and parted. Suddenly from the darkness emerged the wild, snakey hair and staring eyes of a terrifying figurehead. Now the hull slid into view. The vessel towered over them, its tattered sails hanging like cobwebs from the masts. Everything was lit with an eerie green light.

"By the shades," whispered Captain Blade. "We've found our ghost ship!"

Chapter Ten

Sam stared in horror at the hulking ship. It glowed in the fog and strange lights sent weird shadows flickering across the ruined sails. Shimmering seaweed hung in ribbons over the yards. One of the pirates gave a frightened moan while Fernando made the sign of a cross and whispered a prayer. Charlie said nothing but she gripped Sam's arm hard.

Sam wondered if the ghost crew would be see-through spectres or shrieking skeletons. He felt chills running up and down his spine. Crow gave a muffled squawk.

The sight seemed to hold no terrors for the captain. "Sam, lash our boat to their side," he ordered in a low voice. "Follow me, everyone."

He seized the edge of a gun port and swung himself out of the boat without making a sound.

Sam, Charlie and Fernando quickly followed and the crew swarmed behind them up the hull and onto the deck. Everything they touched felt deathly cold and clammy, like a long-forgotten tomb. Each board and rail was covered with the strange gloopy substance that Sam had seen before. Cutlasses drawn, the crew advanced slowly over the mouldering deck. Crow clung to

Sam's shoulder, hiding his head under his wing. Ned held a lantern aloft, sending the light skittering across the boards. The fog oozed around rusting cannon. Broken barrels and rotting rope were strewn about, green and ghostly. It was easy to believe that this ship had festered at the bottom of the sea for years.

"It smells of death," muttered Fernando.

"Let's find the treasure and be on our way," said Ned quickly.

"Aye, before they come out to haunt us," muttered one of his companions.

An unearthly groan filled the air. The crew drew back, huddling together.

"That sounds like a soul in torment," whispered Fernando.

"Look, Captain!" Ned pointed a wobbling finger up at the poop deck.

A figure stood by the broken wheel. It shone with the same strange green glow as the ship. It wore a captain's hat but the face beneath the brim was just bones, the empty eye sockets staring intently at them. The fog billowed . . . and the figure was gone.

"And there's another!" cried Ned.

Now a second phantom appeared on the rigging, the mist swirling about it. And another. Sam could see ghosts materialising all over the ship, each with a ghastly skeletal face. An eerie moaning echoed across the deck.

"Hold your ground, men," said Captain Blade through gritted teeth.

The *Sea Wolf* crew stood uncertainly together.

"How do we defeat these apparitions?" hissed Ned.

"Aye," came another whispered voice. "They are not of this world."

Ned suddenly gave a terrified cry.

"We're all going to die!" he yelled. "See my hands. They're turning green. I'm changing into a ghost!"

"Agghhh! Ned's cursed and so are we!" called one of the pirates, looking at his glowing breeches. He fell to his knees. "Spirits of the deep, have mercy on us."

The *Sea Wolf* crew searched themselves frantically, all finding signs of the deadly glow on their skin and clothes.

"Even you, Captain," cried Fernando.

Captain Blade gazed in horror at his coat. The cuffs and hem were shining ghostly green like the rest. For a moment, Sam felt helpless. If the brave Captain Blade was spooked then there was no hope for the rest of them.

"We'll be dead in minutes," groaned Ned.

Wait a moment, thought Sam. *I've had this stuff on me for hours and I'm not dead. What's going on?*

More ghosts came spilling out of hatches and from behind cannon. They began to creep towards the crew, their moaning growing louder and louder.

Sam was desperate. His shipmates were going to be overcome without a fight if he didn't act now. If this gloop was truly spectral, then surely it would have done something horrible to him already. Yet he felt fine. That meant the gloop wasn't ghostly after all.

In fact this whole scene was beginning to remind him of a ride he'd been on at a theme park. It was called 'Midnight Horror' and you were whisked around on a rollercoaster in the pitch dark while scary things kept appearing. You could see them because they were covered in luminous paint. Had the ghosts got some substance that made them glow in the dark? It couldn't be luminous paint because Sam was pretty sure that hadn't been invented yet, but he'd heard that some seaweed was luminous. And that would explain the fishy smell.

"This ghost ship is nothing but a trick!" he yelled.

He leapt forward and shoved the nearest ghost in the chest. The phantom gave a cry of surprise and fell over backwards.

"Blow the man down!" Crow flapped off Sam's shoulder and took hold of the ghost's skeletal nose with his beak. He

gave it a wrench and the face
came away and smashed
into pieces on the deck.
The spectral crew gave
cries of alarm and shrank back.

"That's no ghost!" yelled Charlie. She
poked the man's leg with her toe. "He's
flesh and blood. He was just wearing a
mask."

"It's all a trick," Sam told his shipmates.
"They've covered themselves with this
gloopy stuff to make them look more like
phantoms. And they've covered the ship
too. So when we climbed on board, we
got it all over us as well. It's completely
harmless – although it does stink."

Captain Blade flashed his cutlass in the
air.

"I am the captain of the *Sea Wolf*," he
cried. "Your ghostly tricks do not scare us.
Hand over your treasure and we'll be on
our way."

The tall ghost pirate in the glowing tricorn hat and hideous mask stepped forward to face him. "And *I* am the captain of the *Queen Caterina*," he growled. "You will be going nowhere. None may know our secret and live."

CHAPTER ELEVEN

The clash of swords rang over the deck as the two crews met in deadly combat. The enemy sent shivers down Sam's spine. He knew that these were no ghosts, yet their sightless eyes and glowing clothes were still terrifying.

There was an unearthly cry and he swung round to see a figure with a deathly grinning mask running at him.

At lightning speed he jumped aside and struck the man's cutlass with his own. It spun in the air. As it came down, Sam caught it deftly by the handle.

Now he had two weapons he could face them all! Whirling the swords round his head he leapt into the fray. The crew of the *Sea Wolf* were fighting bravely, with far more skill than their enemy. But the ghost crew had the advantage – they knew their own ship and they were used to the fog. They could appear and disappear in it as if they really were spectres.

Then, above his head, Sam suddenly spotted Fernando held against the rigging by two ghost pirates. A third held a knife to his throat. Sam leapt into action. He climbed up and slashed at the ropes the villains were standing on. The men fell to the deck with a cry.

"They have the upper hand!" yelled Sam, as he and Fernando clung to the broken rigging.

Fernando turned to him, a glint in his eye. "Not for long," he growled. "Look, their captain is below — and he's a poor fighter indeed. We can take him easily."

The captain of the *Queen Caterina* was down on the deck, fending off an expert attack from Charlie. He was only keeping her at bay with his greater strength.

Fernando took aim and sent his knife spinning down through the air. The handle slammed into the captain's hand. He dropped his sword with a cry and the two boys leapt on to him, pinning him to the deck.

Charlie darted forwards and snatched up his fallen sword.

"Captain Blade!" she yelled. "We have their leader."

A shiver of shock ran through the ghost

pirates. The *Sea Wolf* crew seized the moment. Soon their fearsome-looking enemies were shivering with fear as they were rounded up on the deck.

"Take off your masks!" ordered Captain Blade. "Or are you too cowardly to let us see your faces?" The ghosts obeyed. "Now throw those false faces overboard," went on the captain, "and that will be an end to your low tricks."

"Well, well, well," said Ned, catching one snivelling wretch by the arm and turning his face to the moonlight. "If it isn't Jake Roberts. I remember you. You always were a coward."

"Upon my life their leader is Jeremiah Symes," said Captain Blade with a harsh laugh. "Couldn't fight the skin off a rice pudding. And there are others I remember, too."

"So they're all failed pirates," Sam whispered to Fernando.

"Looks like it," replied his friend, nodding. "They had to hide behind masks in order to be brave."

"Tie up that snivelling band and keep guard on 'em, men," said Captain Blade in a ringing tone. "Fernando, Charlie, Sam, you're with me. We've got treasure to find."

They climbed down the steep steps to the hold and shone their lanterns round. Chests and sacks lay in piles, each one full to the brim with doubloons, jewels

and gold plates. The riches glittered and gleamed in the lantern light.

Fernando gave a low whistle of amazement.

"This is magnificent," said Captain Blade, surveying the hoard.

"It's a shame it won't all fit in our boats," said Charlie. She draped an emerald necklace over her head. "Do we just take a little bit?"

"No, by thunder!" The captain had a broad smile on his face. "We'll simply borrow the ghost ship. Once we reach the *Sea Wolf* and unload the booty, the phantoms can have their ship back. Not that it'll do them much good now that their secret is out!"

The ghost ship was soon ready to leave. The *Sea Wolf* pirates raised the anchor.

Captain Blade strode over to the captured crew. "Which course?" he demanded. "Tell me the currents that will take us out of this infernal fog, for there's no wind."

"I know every current and rock in this fog like the back of my hand," sneered Jeremiah Symes defiantly, "but I'll not be telling you. Not even if you run me through."

"Hmmm," said Blade, fingering his sword thoughtfully. "Now that would be a silly thing for me to do, for a dead man cannot give directions."

"Me lips are sealed!"

"Then I'll make my own course," said Captain Blade jovially. "And if we hit a rock and perish, we'll all be ghosts together."

"What is he doing?" whispered Sam.

"Trust the captain," Fernando whispered back.

Blade took the wheel and spun it hard. The ghost ship began to move forward, pulled by an invisible current.

Fernando, Charlie and Sam were at the bows. They could see that the *Queen Caterina* was heading straight for the rock where the *Falmouth* lay wrecked.

Sam couldn't believe that the captain hadn't seen it. "Rocks ahead!" he yelled.

Captain Blade had a grim look on his face as he held his course. "Aye, aye, Sam Silver," he called. "Prepare for shipwreck!"

The captured crew began to pull at their bonds and beg their leader to give directions.

"Be quiet, you scurvy scabs," he growled. "He'll not sink us. He wants to live as much as we all do."

"You would think so," said Captain Blade pleasantly, "but what life would it be, lost for ever in this accursed fog? No, I'll hold the course and make our end a quick one. We'll be in good company. See, here's the *Falmouth* waiting for us to join her."

The leader of the ghosts began to shift uneasily. Soon the ship would have no time to turn. But Captain Blade stared straight ahead.

"Hard to starboard, darn you!" cried Symes.

The captain had a wry grin on his face as he set the new course. The ghost ship scraped against the rock and then moved on.

"That was close," Sam whispered to Charlie. "For one moment I thought we'd be swimming with the fishes."

"Captain Blade knew what he was doing," said Charlie. "At least, I hope so."

"Stars!" yelled Fernando, pointing up at the night sky. "And the moon. We're coming out of the Cloud of Death! "

"Well I'll be a ship's biscuit," said Ned as they came out into the clear night air. "We've done it. There's the *Sea Wolf*. I've never been more glad to see her."

The vessel lay at anchor in the dark sea some distance from the fog bank, the figurehead gleaming in the moonlight. Fernando shouted a greeting.

"They won't hear you from here, lad," said Captain Blade. "Have patience. We'll soon be alongside."

But suddenly there was a distant boom and a cloud of smoke rose from the *Sea Wolf*'s deck. *Splash!* A cannonball landed close to the *Queen Caterina*.

"They think we're the enemy," gasped Sam. "They're going to sink us!"

CHAPTER TWELVE

As the smoke cleared on the *Sea Wolf*, Sam could see the distant crew hurriedly reloading the cannon.

Boom! Another barrage of cannonballs was on its way. There was a horrible splintering crash as a missile hit the mainmast. The mast smashed down onto the deck.

"We have the best gun crew in the Caribbean," muttered Captain Blade. "Yet I never thought to be on the wrong end of it."

Sam and Charlie darted to the bows, shouting and waving their arms at the *Sea Wolf*. Fernando grabbed a piece of tattered sail, ran to the end of the bowsprit and tried to signal a ceasefire, but the cannonballs kept coming. Ned went down below to check for damage. The ghost crew moaned and strained against their bonds.

"I'll make sure your ropes are cut if the ship sinks," the captain assured them.

"Hoist the signals!" screeched Crow, hunched on Sam's shoulder.

"A signal," gasped Sam. "You're right, Crow. Could you fly over to the ship with a message?"

Captain Blade looked down at his ring with the blood red stone. He pulled it off and tossed it to Sam. "You give it to the . . . crow, lad," he said. "I'm hoping Harry will know that it could only have come from me."

Crow snapped it up in his beak.

"Off you go, Crow," said Sam. "Give this to the first mate."

They watched until the green parrot was only a tiny dot against the sails of the *Sea Wolf*.

"They're reloading, Captain," reported Fernando.

"And we're shipping water faster than we can bail," cried Ned, his head appearing through the hatch.

Clutching the rail, Sam waited for the next cloud of smoke that would show the *Sea Wolf* cannon had fired again. The seconds passed.

"They're coming towards us," yelled Charlie. "They must be getting ready for another bombardment."

"Just as I would have done!" exclaimed Captain Blade. "Upon my life, I've taught them too well."

Everyone held their breath, waiting for the next barrage. The seconds ticked by . . .

"They're not firing, Captain," said Sam.

The *Sea Wolf* continued its course towards them. Now they could make out the faces of their crewmates. They held a mixture of fear and hope. And there was Harry Hopp on the foredeck, peering intently at the *Queen Caterina* through his spyglass, while Crow sat perched on his bald head.

"Is it really you, Captain?" he cried, holding up the ring. "We got your sign from this brave bird here. But you're not a phantom, are you?"

"I'm flesh and blood!" called Blade cheerfully. "As are the crew of this ship. There is no ghost vessel. It was all a trick."

"Then we'll be happy to come alongside," the first mate called back.

The moment they were in reach, Harry ordered ropes to be thrown to lash the two ships together. "It was a chilling sight to watch you go into that infernal fog and see that ghost ship come out," he shouted across, a huge grin splitting his stubbly cheeks. "I feared we'd seen the last of you, me hearties. I should have known better."

"And then that parr . . . crow brought us the message," added Ben. "And we knew you were all right."

"We've had such a time as would make your hair curl," Ned shouted back to them. "It all started with . . ."

"Belay there, Ned," said Captain Blade, slapping him on the back. "Tell the tale later. We've got treasure to load. And make haste. I don't know how long this vessel has above the waves. The *Sea Wolf* cannon fired good and true."

Without the weight of the treasure, the ghost ship looked as if she might limp to the nearby island.

The miserable crew were untied and left to sail their damaged ship as best they could. The *Sea Wolf* caught the wind and set off.

"North north-east!" called Captain Blade. "It's a long voyage but I've a yearning to see our hideout on Skeleton Island again. This time we'll stow some of our treasure and not spend it all."

"Aye," agreed Harry Hopp. "And we'll have a grand celebration there."

Sam put a hand on the rigging, ready to take up his lookout duty. Crow flapped on to his shoulder.

"Pieces of eight!" he squawked.

Captain Blade looked over sharply.

Sam's heart sank with a thud. He remembered the captain's words. Crow would be gone the next time he came back to the *Sea Wolf*.

The captain cleared his throat. "That . . . crow has proved himself a loyal crew member," he said, keeping his distance. "We owe him our lives. He may stay on board."

"Thank you, Captain!" exclaimed Sam, going forward to shake his hand.

"Not so fast there, lad!" cried Captain Blade, jumping back smartly. "The bird can stay . . . as far away from me as possible."

"Aye, aye, Captain," said Sam happily. He turned to Charlie and Fernando, a big smile on his face.

"High five!" yelled Fernando, holding up his palm to Sam. "And this time I promise not to break your fingers."

The three friends high fived and Crow nearly fell off Sam's shoulder.

"Stormy seas!" he shrieked.

Sam suddenly wondered what would happen to the parrot when he wasn't there.

"Will you look after Crow for me, Charlie," he asked, "when I go back . . . to see my mum?"

"I would, but I don't think Sinbad would be very happy about that," said Charlie.

"I'll take care of him," said Fernando. Sam grinned and thanked his friend, and suddenly he felt a strange tingling in his fingers and toes. He knew what that meant – he was about to be whisked back home. But he couldn't disappear in front of Fernando!

"I've left my spyglass below," he gabbled. He threw himself down the steps to the storeroom but already everything was spinning around him. In another moment, the familiar dark tunnel had sucked him in and deposited him on his bedroom carpet in the flat above the fish and chip shop.

Sam quickly jumped to his feet and scrambled into his school uniform. He found he didn't mind so much about the football-free week now. He'd had a brilliant time on the *Sea Wolf*, chasing ghost ships and plundering treasure, and he knew he could go back to his crew whenever he wanted.

But best of all, the *Sea Wolf* had got its

own permanent pirate parrot . . . or crow,
if Captain Blade was in sight!

CREW MANIFEST

Sinbad

Crow

Thomas Blade
Captain

Peter Craddock
Ship's Cook

Fernando
Rigger

Don't miss the next exciting adventure in the
Sam Silver: Undercover Pirate series

Kidnapped

Available in August 2012!
Read on for a special preview
of the first chapter.

CHAPTER ONE

Sam Silver picked up his football and
raced out of his bedroom. He was
off to the beach for an important match
with his friends and there wasn't a
minute to spare. He made for the stairs
that led from the flat to his parents'
fish and chip shop below.

Thump! He collided with
something solid that grunted.

It was his dad.

"Watch it, Sam!" said his father, staggering back on to the dirty-washing basket. "Why are you in your football kit? Hurry up and change. Arnold will be here in a minute."

Sam nearly dropped his football in horror. He'd forgotten all about Arnold. His mother's cousin was the most boring person in the whole world, if not in the whole universe. Mum always made him dress up in his smartest clothes when Arnold visited and it was impossible to sit still and listen while Arnold droned on and on.

"I have to go down to the beach," he protested. "I've got a really important game with my mates."

"You can't play football when Arnold's coming," insisted his dad. "You know he'll be upset if you're not here. Now get changed."

Sam mooched back into his bedroom and pulled out his best shirt and trousers. He wondered what Cousin Arnold would lecture them about this time. Bee-keeping in Tudor England? Which toothpicks the ancient Egyptians used? Knitting in the Middle Ages? Arnold knew loads about history and managed to make it all sound really boring.

Well, Sam knew something Arnold didn't know. He knew how it felt to travel back three hundred years in time to a pirate ship in the Caribbean and have awesome adventures. It was Sam's big secret. One day he'd found an old glass bottle, washed up on the beach of his home in Backwater Bay. Inside was a gold coin sent by Joseph Silver, Sam's pirate ancestor. It had been filthy so he'd tried to clean it with a bit of spit and a rub. The next thing he knew he'd found himself aboard a real pirate ship, the *Sea Wolf*, with Captain Blade and his band of fearsome buccaneers.

Sam tried to imagine Arnold on board the *Sea Wolf*. It would be a disaster. Arnold would bore the crew so much they'd all be fighting to walk the plank after five minutes!

An idea suddenly catapulted into Sam's brain. Arnold might not be welcome on the pirate ship – but Sam knew the crew would be delighted to see *him*! And, as no time ever passed when he slipped off to the Caribbean, he could have a swashbuckling adventure and still be back in time for Arnold's visit.

Sam threw down his smart clothes and quickly put on the scruffy T-shirt, jeans and trainers he always wore for his time travelling. He couldn't risk coming back from an adventure with his best shirt and trousers dirty and ripped.

He carefully took the bottle from the collection of beach treasures displayed on his shelf and shook out the gold coin. He spat on the doubloon – Silver Spit seemed to be the magic ingredient – and rubbed it on his sleeve.

"*Sea Wolf*, here I come!" he yelled.

There was a loud rushing sound and Sam felt as if he were caught in a whirlwind. The furniture set off in a wild spin round his head. Sam closed his eyes tightly. He didn't want to get time-travel sickness. When the spinning stopped he felt himself land on a hard wooden floor. He could smell rope and tar and hot, salty air. He opened his eyes. Great! He was back in the little storeroom on the *Sea Wolf*. He rammed his coin deep in his back pocket.

A tatty jerkin, belt and a spyglass – an old-fashioned telescope – lay in a heap on a barrel. His friend, Charlie, must have put them there, ready for his next appearance. She was the only one who knew his time-travelling secret.

A black cat was curled up on top of the pile. It opened one eye and gave him an evil stare.

"Good boy, Sinbad," Sam said nervously, trying to edge forward.

Merow! A set of vicious claws flashed out. Sam leapt back.

Sinbad, the ship's cat, was fiercely loyal to the crew. And fierce was the word. None of the pirates dared go near

him except for Charlie. The mangy cat adored her and turned into a purring ball of fur whenever she was near.

Sinbad arched his back, gave a hiss and leapt out of the door.

Before the cat could change his mind, Sam quickly put on the jerkin and belt and grabbed his spyglass.

Now he was ready for action!